Original title: O regresso
Copyright © Bruaá Editora, 2014
Published in Canada and the USA in 2019 by Groundwood Books

Groundwood Books / House of Anansi Press
groundwoodbooks.com

We gratefully acknowledge the Government of Canada for its financial
support of our publishing program.

With the participation of the Government of Canada
Avec la participation du gouvernement du Canada | Canadä

Library and Archives Canada Cataloguing in Publication
Title: The return / Natalia Chernysheva.
Other titles: Regresso. English | Retour.
Names: Chernysheva, Natalia, author, illustrator.
Description: Translation of: O Regresso. | Adaptation from the short film
Le retour, directed by Natalia Chernysheva.
Identifiers: Canadiana (print) 20189065850 | Canadiana (ebook)
20189065869 | ISBN 9781773062099 (hardcover) |
ISBN 9781773062105 (EPUB) | ISBN 9781773062839 (Kindle)
Classification: LCC PZ7.1.C533 Ret 2019 | DDC j869.3/5—dc23

The illustrations were done in Chinese ink and monoprint,
with colors added digitally in TVPaint.
Design by Cláudia Lopes
Printed and bound in Malaysia

THE RETURN

Natalia Chernysheva

Groundwood Books
House of Anansi Press
Toronto   Berkeley

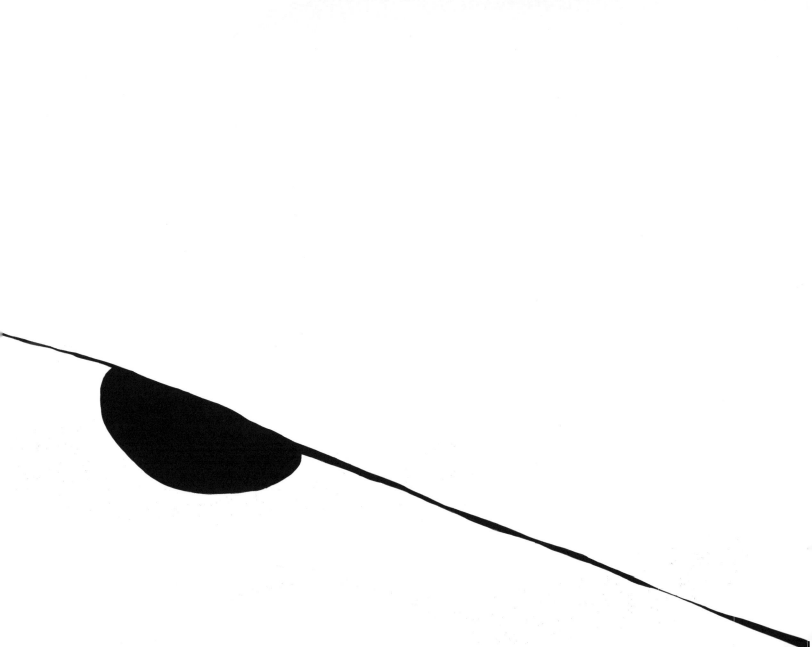